MW01705150

Flash in the Can

Number One

"In-house, outhouse or at the Ritz, "Flash in the Can" is a great collection of flush fiction! You'll want to take a copy with you wherever you go!"

Ruth M. McCarty, author of murder mysteries and 2009 Derringer Winner for Flash Fiction

"Creative flash fiction from front to back."

Randall DeWitt, award-winning flash fiction author

"This delightful collection of flash crime fiction is like a box of your favorite chocolates. Dip in, enjoy, and dip in again. Perfect for carrying in your purse or on your device to kill the boredom of waiting, perhaps in the company of a mischievous garden gnome. What better remedy for life's frustrations than a little murder, mayhem, or revenge?"

Kate Flora, award-winning author of the Joe Burgess and Thea Kozak mystery series

Flash in the Can Number One

By
Diane Kane
and
Kathy Chencharik

A book of short stories
to read wherever you go.

With featured stories
by authors
Phyllis Cochran
and
Sharon A. Harmon

ISBN: 13:978-1-7323973-0-9

First Edition: September 2018

Cover Design by the flashy Cindy Rieth

Copy editing by the canny Diane Hinckley

Library of Congress Control Number: 2018910289

Dedicated to

the imagination of dreamers and all the writers who entertain their characters on the written page.

All photos of this outhouse taken at
Rock Ridge Farm
Northfield, MA

Flash Fiction

Aka: Flush Fiction

As Flash Fiction writers, we follow in the ancient footsteps of the creators of fables and fairy tales. We take the ordinary happenings of life and blend them with magic in 1,500 words or less. Perfect to read in just one flush.

Table of Contents

TAKING CARE OF BUSINESS

Diane Kane

The starchy county clerk in Girdwood, Alaska, looked at me with contempt as she signed the temporary land claim form.

"Everybody knows there isn't any gold in Crow Creek," she said.

"Why's that?" I asked. Alaska was the land of gold. I figured Crow Creek had its share and she just didn't take kindly to strangers finding it.

"Ask Horace Heald when you see him," she said as she cackled like a hen well past her laying years. Adjusting my hat to cover my flushing face, I handed over the hundred thirty-five-dollar fee, snatched the form from her desk, and exited.

That afternoon when I went out to Crow Creek to mark my claim, I met Horace, or at least I saw him. He silently followed me around, his thumbs hooked around his frayed suspenders, chewing on a wad of tobacco.

With plot map in hand, I walked his boundary line. Stopping, I grabbed the mallet from my back pocket and pounded a stake into the ground, legally marking the northeast corner of my claim. Horace peered over my shoulder. I stood up, and Horace jumped back.

"I'm here for the summer," I said. "I hope we can become friends."

He looked me in the eye, and spat brown fluid out the side of his mouth, wiping the excess from his lips with the sleeve of his tattered red-and-black wool coat. He turned and trudged up the slight incline toward a weather-beaten outhouse. The rusty hinges creaked when he opened the faded wooden door with a half-moon cutout. He gave it a hefty slam, and the tin roof rattled.

There was no sign of Horace the next day when I hiked in with my supplies. Setting up camp, I kept an eye out. Finally, I spied him up on the ridge beside the outhouse with his old shotgun in the crook of his arm. I hadn't brought a weapon, but I held up my can of bear mace. He shook his head with a grin.

Horace was a quiet man, but he kept a close eye on me. He squatted on a rock nearby while I set up my tent. Later in the day when a sockeye salmon bit the fly on the end of my line, Horace nodded in approval. That night I skewered the fish and roasted it over the campfire. Horace hovered by the creek. I motioned him over, but he tipped his floppy hat and faded into the woods.

I wasn’t sure where Horace slept, but I always knew when he came to the outhouse by the sound of the creaking hinges on the wormwood pine door. I never used the shed myself. It was on Horace's claim, so I did my business in the great outdoors.

Day after day, I dug buckets of dirt from the sides of the creek and sifted them through my portable sieve. Swishing the black soil around my emerald green plastic pan, I’d pour it slowly over the rows of raised ridges. Each time I got to the bottom of the pan, I swirled the last bits of sand around in the cold creek water, in hopes of seeing a shining nugget of gold. Time after time, I threw out the lackluster dirt that stared back at me.

I wouldn’t say that Horace and I became close friends, but I felt like we developed a respect for each other. Not far up the river from me, Horace worked meticulously with his homemade wooden sluice and rusty old metal pan. Observing Horace, I admired his patient manner and grew fond of the lines around his sullen eyes. I’d wave my hand at him and took pleasure in his acknowledging toothless grin.

The snowmelt in the Chugach Mountain Range lessened over the next month, and the flow of the water slowed. One morning I decided to take a break from my fruitless gold panning and go for a hike to clear my mind.

I crossed the dwindling creek to the opposite shore and caught a trail that snaked up a steep incline. I hadn't gone far when I heard someone approaching through the brush. I knew it was Horace, curious about what I was up to, and content to follow behind. Near the crest of the ridge, I stopped to catch my ragged breath and marveled as I heard the snap of a branch, signaling that the old prospector was still on my tail.

Across the valley, thunder rumbled, and I knew I'd better start my descent. The summer storms came fast through the valley, and I didn't want to get caught in this storm's wrath unprepared. I started down the mountain thinking I would meet Horace on the trail.

Instead, I discovered that my pursuer was an enormous grizzly. I stopped dead in my tracks, grabbing at my side for the bear mace that I had left back at camp. The bear rose up on his rear legs and twisted his head in a ferocious roar. I fell to the ground, clawing my way backward in the dirt. Without warning, the grizzly froze, his eyes got big, and he let out a cry like a scared child. Dropping to his four paws, he ran full bore, crashing through the woods as if his tail was on fire. I was lying in the path trembling when I heard a chuckle behind me.

"How did you do that?" I asked, smiling up at Horace.

He didn't have time to answer before the hail started to pelt down with fury. Jagged streaks of lightning lit the sky, immediately followed by the deafening roar of thunder. I looked back for Horace as I stumbled down the path to the river. With my heart pounding, I waited beside the creek for Horace to appear from the trail.

I couldn't believe my eyes when I glimpsed him on the other side of the water. Somehow, he had passed me and was running into the outhouse.

Thunder drummed through my chest, while the lightning current sang like a soprano across the tin roof on the outhouse. Sparks snapped, giving life to flames that danced on the dried-out wood. I ran toward the little building, with the wild weather drowning my screams. I was about fifty yards away when the house exploded. I ducked behind a tree as falling pieces of outhouse debris mixed with the sheets of torrential rain poured down on me.

The storm cleared as fast as it came. I meandered among the smoldering pieces of wood looking for any sign of Horace. It was if he had disappeared into thin air. Kicking the rusty hinges lying on the ground amid the rubble, I exposed a gaping hole. I thought it must be the remnants of the latrine until I notice the contents shimmering in the shafts of emerging sunlight. Peering into the cavity, I found the mother lode. Horace had done a lot of business in the outhouse. The business of buried treasure.

***

The cocky sheriff was leaning over the county clerk's desk when I walked into the office. They frowned at me like a fly on the potato salad at a picnic.

"I've come to turn in my claim," I said as I handed her the water-stained paper.

"Still another couple months of summer." The sheriff grinned. "Prospecting gold not all you thought it would be?"

I ignored the sheriff's rebuff and turned toward him. "I was planning to visit your office next."

He stood up to his full six-foot-plus height. "Why's that, boy?"

"The storm that passed through this morning hit hard out at the camp," I said. "There was an accident."

His eyes squinted. "I heard the thunder rolling through the valley. Sounded like the lightning made a big strike out near the creek."

"It hit the tin roof on the outhouse." I swallowed hard. "The dry wood caught fire, and it must have sparked an old store of ammo." I hesitated. "Horace was in there."

The sheriff's eyebrows shot halfway up his forehead.

"It's the truth," I said. "When the storm cleared, I sifted through the remnants of the scattered house, but I didn't find any signs of Horace."

The sheriff bent over clutching his stomach, as he roared with laughter. The county clerk grabbed for a tissue to soak up the tears of mirth streaming down her cheeks.

I stood bewildered by their reactions. The sheriff choked back his laughter. "Horace Heald's been dead going on twenty years." He paused. "Died right there at Crow Creek." His face sobered. "They didn't find a flake of gold on him."

"You look like you've seen a ghost." The county clerk's voice echoed in my ears, and a shiver crawled up my spine.

I quickly processed this new revelation. "I was just joking," I said, trying to keep my wits.

"Did the ghost of Horace happen to show you any gold?" The sheriff's eyes narrowed.

I shook my head and smiled. "Everyone knows there isn't any gold in Crow Creek."

GHOST COACH

Kathy Chencharik

"Tell us a story, Angie!" the twins pleaded, their white dresses covered in specks of dirt. As they sat in the doorway of the old abandoned building, lightning flashed, thunder rumbled, and it began to rain. Ten-year-old Angie smiled.

"A long time ago," she began, gazing into their dark brown eyes, "a man named Aldo Bolini lived in this building. He was a peddler who sold wares from a coach pulled by two black horses. One rainy day, just like today, he was driving home and was ambushed. He was robbed and murdered." Angie slowly slid a finger across her throat. The twins cringed.

"The murderers," she continued, "draped a tarp across the front of the coach to hide his body. His horses brought him home. Even today, people in the village have said they've seen the ghost coach and two black horses stop in front of this doorway."

The twins glanced outside. The rain came down harder. Soon, they heard the sound of hoofbeats reverberating along the cobblestone street. The twins jumped up and peered around the doorway. A tarp-draped coach, pulled by two black horses, rounded the corner. The twins screamed and ran through the rain toward home.

"What's wrong with them?" a man asked as he stopped in front of the doorway. "You'd think they just saw a ghost."

Angie shrugged her shoulders, lifted the tarp, and climbed inside.

"By the way, Angie, that was a great idea you had of using a tarp," he said. "It keeps me nice and dry in the rain. Am I late?"

"No, Papa, you're right on time," she said with a smile.

GNOME SWEET GNOME

Diane Kane

Every year I dread Thanksgiving dinner at Aunt Sheila's. I spend the entire hour-and-forty-three-minute trip stressing about my hair, my weight, my year's accomplishments or, more to the point, the lack thereof. As a single freelance writer without a boyfriend, a steady paycheck, or a 401K, I feel like the black sheep of my overachieving family. Since both my parents passed away, Aunt Sheila and her brood are my only blood relatives, even if their blood is a little richer than mine.

In the parking lot of the Speedy Mart on the corner of Main and Primrose Drive, just down the hill from my aunt's house, I suck on the last cigarette to touch my lips for the next four hours. Blowing the smoke away from my clothes, I spray myself with a healthy dose of perfume and reluctantly drive up the hill.

Aunt Sheila lives in a grand Victorian perfectly restored to its former historical elegance. Her daughter Catherine married into old money. She and her husband Taylor spawned a set of identical twin girls, Makayla and Michaela. Aunt Sheila's son William looks like

Prince Charming, and his wife, Stella, is an underwear model. The perfect couple has one perfect son, Young Willy.

Approaching Aunt Sheila's sprawling porch, I hesitate and look down at the old weathered garden gnome beside the step.

"I'm surprised they keep you around," I sneer. "You look as out of place here as I do."

I hear a raspy chuckle as I trip on the last stair, slamming my head into the solid oak door. Aunt Sheila swings the door open wide and wipes her hands in the folds of her flowered apron. Smells of roasting turkey and homemade spiced-applesauce escape into the chilled air.

"What are you doing hanging around on the front porch, Rebecca?" Aunt Sheila grabs my right hand as I rub the bump on my head with my left.

"I tripped—." I began.

"Was it a good trip here?"

"Yes, but I think your gnome—."

"Don't be silly, Becky, of course I'm home; it's Thanksgiving." Aunt Sheila motions me inside. "We're all waiting for you."

I give up trying to explain to Aunt Sheila; but it's probably for the best. My head starts to clear from my collision with the door, and I laugh to myself at the idea that the gnome had anything to do with it. My cousins give me quick pecks on the cheek as they buzz back and forth attending to festive details.

"Can I help?" I call out to Catherine.

"We've got this, Becky. Why don't you take the children outside to play?"

Catherine and Taylor's twins, Makayla and Michaela, stare at me with eerie unblinking eyes, while William and Stella's hellion, Young Willy, tries to lasso my legs. Using my childhood ballerina skills, I twirl out of his snare and run into the bathroom. Slamming the door hard, I lock it, turn and slump to the floor. In front of me stands the gnome with a smug look on his chubby face.

"Ahh!" I scream. "What are you doing in here?"

He glances at the bathroom window, and I notice the English ivy growing up the trellis on the outside. A long vine pokes suspiciously through the window and hangs to the floor.

"I was here first." His thick beard and mustache puff out like a hairy blowfish. "I came in to get away from those wild animals they call children."

"Me too!" I confide. "They are the devil's own, aren't they?"

"Catherine and William were no angels when they were young, if I remember correctly," he chuckles.

"You're right." I concede and shake my head. "Wait a minute—I can't really be talking to you."

"Why not? It's better than being out there, isn't it?" he says, flipping his stubby thumb toward the door behind me.

"But you're a little gnome!"

"They always say that you're unorthodox, but I never thought you could be so mean." He looked down and shuffled his tiny feet. "I am short, but short people have feelings too, you know."

"I'm so sorry. I didn't mean to insult you. I was only stating the obvious." He looks at me with sad eyes. "Oh, don't get all sappy. I didn't mean it," I say and pause with revelation. "Who says I'm unorthodox?"

His blue eyes sparkle. "Why, Sheila and William do, and especially Catherine," he whispers. "I hear them talking when they sit on the porch." A mischievous smile lights his face. "They don't know that I can hear them."

"I knew they didn't like me."

"I wouldn't say they don't like you." He wrinkles his forehead. "I think they're jealous of you." He nods his head with certainty.

"Jealous of me?" I eye him skeptically.

"Oh, yes," he assures me. "Catherine sometimes wishes to be free from her demanding husband and the needy look-alikes. She would like to have more time to herself as you do."

"Those twins give me the creeps!"

"And William, he hates being tied to his boring accounting job and the stress of making enough money to keep his model wife happy. He dreams of having the freedom of a job like yours."

"What about Aunt Sheila?"

"She talks to herself a lot while she's working in the garden." His nose twitches. "She wishes that her children could be more fun-loving and spontaneous like you."

"Really?" I beam. "I think I like you!"

His carefully groomed beard parts wide to reveal two rows of straight white teeth.

I jump up at the pounding on the door. “Becky, are you all right?” Catherine shouts. “We heard you scream.”

“Let us in.” Aunt Sheila’s voice is full of concern.

The portly gnome shuffles into the linen closet as I unlock the door. “I’m fine,” I assure them.

“We were worried.” William pushes in with all the little urchins behind him. “Who were you talking to?”

They all scan the empty bathroom with confusion.

“I was just having a little talk with myself.” A nervous laugh sticks in my throat on seeing one of the twins peer into the closet.

“This is our gnome!” the nasty little child yells as she holds the ceramic statue precariously by its little red boots.

“Be careful with him,” I shout.

“You were trying to steal our gnome,” she cries. The whole family simultaneously turns toward me.

"If you wanted the gnome, Rebecca," Aunt Sheila says with raised eyebrows, "you could have just asked for it."

"I don't want the gnome," I say as I grab the statue away from the twin. "I noticed he's dirty. I want to wash him up, that's all."

I look at the inanimate figure in my hand and question my sanity when I feel the little bugger vibrate. The smoke alarm goes off, and everyone runs to the kitchen.

"Thanks for rescuing me from that crazy kid," Gnome smirks once we're alone.

"I'm not at all sure who the crazy one is here, but you are going back out to the garden where you belong."

"How about that bath you promised first?"

I run his head under the cold water and place him gently outside next to the step.

"A little grease drippings on the bottom of the oven, but no harm was done," Aunt Sheila says as we sit down to the dinner table.

"Thank you for cleaning our gnome, Auntie Becky," says Makayla…or Michaela.

I look at her with shock. I wasn't aware she even knew my name. "You're welcome, hum, Mmm…"

"Michaela," she says sweetly. I eye her warily.

Steaming bowls of sweet potato and stuffing pass around the polished oak table. The conversation rewinds to my childhood visits to Aunt Sheila's. The lively accounts of mischievous adventures with William and Catherine put me in good spirits. The fine wine doesn't hurt my outlook, either. I hold up my long-stemmed crystal goblet in a toast to my not-so-perfect family and almost feel like I belong.

At the end of the long day, William helps me on with my coat as we all exchange hugs and kisses. The children shout, "Bye, bye, Auntie Becky!" and it gives me a chill.

Outside alone, I pause at the bottom of the stairs. Gnome stands precisely where I placed him, straight-faced and rigid, with his hands tucked stiffly behind his back. Inhaling the crisp autumn air, I shake my head.

"Well, this has been a strange day," I say to myself as I hurry down the brick path to my car and a much-needed cigarette. A raspy little chuckle ripples through the breeze, as I trip on an invisible obstacle. I glare back at the gnome and swear I see his little whiskers twitching.

DEAL OR NO DEAL

Sharon Harmon

"Dan the Man" ran his hand through his nondescript muddy brown hair then fixed his cool blue eyes onto yet another Pabst Blue Ribbon. His fake gold chains clinked as he kicked his way across a floor littered with empty containers from fast food dives.

A brisk breeze seeped around the windowpanes, and the smell of steam hissed through the radiators in tune with the never-ending clanking of inconsistent heat in the pipes. Dan had been in this little hellhole of a rundown town on the outskirts of Manchester, New Hampshire, for almost a year now. Surfing the channels of an old console television, Dan's eyes glazed over as he watched soap operas and reality shows like "Lifestyles of the Rich and Famous."

"What a car, what a house, what beautiful bitches," Dan mumbled to himself. He pictured having a bright yellow Corvette and a buxom blonde with heavy makeup and 5-inch stilettos hanging on his arm.

Shifting his bony butt on the cracked and worn fake leather couch, he clicked back to the news, anxiously seeking the weather report. Dan lit up yet another hand-rolled cigarette without noticing that the ashtray was already overflowing.

This time would be different, he had thought. *Maybe my ship will come in.*

He dreamed of making his way down the coast to some little town in Florida, in a snazzy car. He would get all the chicks and booze he wanted.

For months, he had double-talked tired and timid couples, or single loser guys like himself, into how his wonderful and affordable used cars would enhance their lives.

In the spring, he had hung lots of bright balloons and even placed a small ad in the local newspaper offering free lollipops and popcorn at his grand opening. For $500.00 down, all your dreams could come true. He boasted that a trusty car from his lot could "get you to work, get your kids to school, and even get you out a night or two. What a deal!"

Dan vehemently shook the hands of single men and commented on the hooters of the cute chicks coming out of the Burger King across the road. He winked a lot as he discussed the best honky-tonk bars to score. The stream of losers, wannabes, and con men came through weekly. He wore the same suit day in and day out, trying to look suave and professional as he wove them under his spell.

He clicked through the stations again and found the news. He looked at the luscious anchorwoman and settled down to listen. “Another local man seems to be missing; this makes seven since late last fall. Authorities are still searching for the men. Stay tuned for more.” Dan tapped his foot repeatedly waiting for the weather.

“Now a weather report from Harvey,” said the blonde newsgirl, her white teeth and sparkly earrings flashing.

Harvey appeared on the screen in his sharp suit, cleanly shaved. “I think you’re gonna like this report, folks,” he said beaming. “There just might be a late January thaw headed this way. Temperatures may reach the low 60s.”

Dan jumped to his feet, grabbed his thin jacket, and drove the four blocks to his used car lot. It was 6:30, and as usual, the town was dreary and closed up for the evening. For the past three months, the cars on the lot had sat encrusted in snow. Ice storm after ice storm had meant zero sales. He started to feel a springtime breeze on the back of his neck. Rivulets of water and snow slid down the side windows of each car he scraped. He peered in at the blanketed humps in the back seats of two of the vehicles. He had only spent $500.00 of the thirty-five hundred.

Amazing how you could sometimes hide things in plain sight, he thought, as the fog rolled in and he ran to his car.

"Time to get out of Dodge."

ONCE UPON A LUNCH BREAK

Phyllis Cochran

During a lunch break, Deidre and Mary strolled down the main street of Fitchburg. The day was overcast, so they had brought their umbrellas to work. A short distance into the walk, they noticed a few drops of rain. In seconds it was pouring. The two women ducked into a storefront, opened their umbrellas, and continued on.

"Wow, that was quite a cloudburst," Deidre said.

"But look, the street up ahead is completely dry," Mary pointed out.

They turned around and saw that only one section of the sidewalk was wet. When they looked upward, a man on the rooftop was staring down at them, smiling.

He kept right on hosing down the brick building.

SCOOTER TIMES

Diane Kane

While I was driving through town on my way to the grocery store, something strange caught my eye. On the common in the center sits a memorial with a large statue of a Revolutionary War soldier holding a musket. I'd seen it hundreds of times, but today there was something curious circling the base of the statue. I pulled my car over to the side of the road and waited for it to come around again.

I looked with puzzlement at a motorized handicapped three-wheeled scooter creeping around the monument. Squinting in disbelief, I realized the person on the trike was none other than my ninety-two-year-old uncle Otto. I got out of my car and ran across the road, waving my arms to get his attention. It was no use calling his name since he was hard of hearing. His face lit up when he spotted me. Racing in my direction, tearing up the grass, he swerved and came to an abrupt stop beside me.

"Diane, hurry, get on the back," he said. "We have to get out of here before they capture us." I considered if Uncle Otto had lost his mind when I saw a group of scooters similar to his charging in our

direction. I jumped on the back of the one-seater and held on for dear life. We took some quick turns and outmaneuvered our pursuers. Uncle Otto came to a sudden halt behind the dumpster at the elderly housing project where he lived.

"Whew, that was a close one!" he said.

I peeled myself off the back of the seat and brushed the dust from my pants. "What was that all about, Uncle Otto?"

"Those old coots aren't satisfied with the scooters I sold them," he said. "They got together and formed a militia. If they think they can take me down, they got another think coming."

"But, Uncle Otto, they know where you live."

"Oh, a group of them tried camping out by my door, but I held my ground. They fell asleep, and I hurried right past them."

"Be careful, okay?"

"Don't you worry about me, Diane. I'm a veteran, you know."

I kissed my uncle and started walking the two miles back up the hill to where I had left my car. On my way, I saw the senior scooter squad coming down the road toward me in a slow procession. The seniors grumbled, and I heard Uncle Otto's name more than a few times as they crawled past me on their worn-out rides.

Just when I thought I'd gotten by them without notice, I heard someone say, "Hey, that's Otto's niece!"

"Hi, guys. How's it going?" Negative feedback bombarded me. "Okay, tell me what's wrong, so I can try to help."

The mob calmed a little, and they let Henry be their spokesman.

"Diane, we bought these scooters from Otto. He swore they were all in top-notch condition. He told us he went through them with a fine-tooth comb. More like a toilet brush, if you ask me. Every one of them has problems."

The seniors all chimed in with their individual problems.

"Mine won't go over four miles an hour uphill or downhill," said a guy with a black cowboy hat.

"This one won't keep a charge," said the man in a red sweat suit. "It died at the McDonald's drive-thru the other day. The manager had to come out and push me to the side."

Their stories poured out all at once until I put up my hands in surrender. “Let me look into this. I promise I’ll do something.”

I appeased the group for the moment, and they rode away on their broken-down rides. I walked the rest of the way up the hill wondering what the heck I was going to do.

Thinking it over on the ride home, I decided that my first plan of action was to call Uncle Otto’s grandson Donnie. He lived a couple of hours away, but he visited Uncle Otto once a week. I wondered if he knew about the scooter warfare.

“Hi, Donnie, I’m calling about Uncle Otto.”

“Uh-oh, what’s he up to now?”

I told Donnie about the low-speed chase through town. Then I filled him in on the scooter complaints. There was silence on the line. I thought I had lost him when I finally heard a deep sigh.

“He asked me for some tools, and I brought them over to him. He had scooter parts all over his living room. The last time I was there the couch was missing. He told me he sold it. He needed more room to fix scooters and no one sat on the couch anyway.”

"I'd see him with a new scooter almost every month, but I never thought to ask what he was doing with the old ones."

"Each time he would get a new one, he said it wasn't fast enough and he'd order a different model. He had a sizable collection of various motorized chairs when he got the idea to tune them up and sell them to his neighbors in the senior housing project. It was keeping him busy, and I didn't think it would cause any harm," Donnie said.

"It sounds like a good idea, but it seems that Uncle Otto is a better thinker than a mechanic. We better do something before someone gets hurt."

Donnie agreed, so we put our heads together on how best to resolve this scooter dilemma.

Donnie had grown up and gone to school in town. He had a friend named Gary who ran a garage and could fix just about anything. Donnie contacted Gary, and his old classmate was glad to help.

In the meantime, I talked with Sergeant Kershaw of the town police department. The police officer was already aware of the problem. He told me of an incident a few weeks ago.

"The scooter squad was chasing Otto when his scooter battery died," the sergeant said. "I was about to intervene when Otto flagged down a passing pickup. The young men in the truck picked up his scooter with him on it and put it in the back of the pickup. The seniors chased after them but didn't get far." He shook his head. "This is getting serious."

I told him that I was working with Otto's grandson to resolve the problem. I promised that we would get all the scooters fixed to everyone's satisfaction, but I needed a favor from the sergeant to help the disgruntled group move on. I told him my idea, and he was all for it.

The next weekend, Donnie and I escorted the scooter squad to Gary's garage. Gary listened patiently to all their complaints. He wrote down the list of problems and promised he would get them all in tip-top shape. Before we left to bring the seniors back to the project, we took Gary aside and asked him if he could get them all done in two weeks. Gary shook his head, but when we told him why he smiled and said he'd do it.

Two weeks went by without incident. Donnie and I got the scooter squad together and drove them to the garage. When Gary opened up the overhead door, there were ooh's, and aah's from the elderly group. Not only had Gary tuned them up, but he had also polished them and placed an American flag on the back of each one.

Sergeant Kershaw pulled up in his police car. He got out and solemnly inspected each scooter. Turning to the seniors, he declared that they all were the guests of honor in the Veterans Day parade.

The seniors cheered as they jumped on their scooters and turned the keys. Sergeant Kershaw turned on the flashing lights of his police car, and they all lined up behind him. Suddenly, Henry jumped off his scooter and ran over to us.

"We can't do this without Otto," he said.

"Otto, Otto, Otto…," the scooter squad started chanting.

Donnie turned and looked at me with astonishment.

"One of the blessings of having a short memory is never having to hold a grudge," I said with a smile.

Uncle Otto mysteriously drove out from behind the garage and was escorted to the front of the line. Sergeant Kershaw blared the siren, and they all paraded through the streets lined with an admiring crowd of town residents.

All else was long forgotten, and Uncle Otto was known thereafter as the scooter hero.

THE RUNNER

Kathy Chencharik

My husband Mike was a runner. He ran the Boston Marathon. He ran for himself. He ran my life. And then he ran into the arms of another woman. A cute little blue-eyed blonde named Cindy who owned a Chevy pickup truck.

I'm not sure who picked up whom first, but it doesn't matter. The fact is I'd been following them and knew every Boston bar they frequented and when. I knew where she lived and where she parked her truck.

One day I called my mother in New Hampshire. She told me she'd be staying overnight in the hospital for some tests. Perfect.

From a pay phone, I called Cindy. I informed her that Mike had been cheating on her with another woman. In disguise, I went to the bar, added some poison to his drink, and watched the fireworks along with everyone else. Cindy left. I helped him outside. After he succumbed to the poison, I needed to dispose of his body. I figured dismemberment would be the easiest way.

Around midnight, I stopped by Cindy's place. "What did you say, Mike? Need a leg up? No problem."

I hung his leg over the tailgate of Cindy's truck, and then proceeded to the Charles River to dump the rest of him.

The next morning I called Mike and left a message that my mother was in the hospital. I said I wished he'd been home when I headed out last night, but I was in such a hurry I forgot to leave a note.

If my plan doesn't work, soon it will be me who's doing the running, running from the law.

LAST LAP

Diane Kane

The first time I saw Bella, her alluring eyes pierced my soul. Desire burned in the pit of my stomach. I had to have her. Her body language said that she wanted me too. There was just one unpleasant obstacle in our path to bliss. Bella's aging mother was part of the deal.

Bella couldn't leave her behind. So, we all moved together into my ten-room Victorian home. I gave Mummy a large room on the third floor with a plush bed, adorned with antique quilts and lace pillows. Her window looked out over the backyard where she could watch the birds flutter around the feeder. If only the old crone could have been content, but she never seemed happy.

My life with Bella was worth any sacrifice. When she looked into my eyes, I felt her passion. As Bella and I grew closer, Mummy's behavior became more obscure. Often I found her rummaging through boxes in the basement or searching in the rubbish of the laundry room. I tried to ignore the elder's odd quirks, but she only grew more irritating.

Mummy would doze all day in the rocking chair in the parlor. Watching the shallow rise and fall of her sagging chest, I silently wished each breath to be her last. At night, the old biddy roamed the long halls and empty rooms of the large house. I'd wake to heavy footfalls and the creaking of old floorboards, wondering how her slight body could produce such loud effects. Bella slept beside me undisturbed by Mummy's nightly haunts, while I tossed and turned. I despised her wretched existence.

Bella and I had breakfast each morning on the east-facing porch. I drank in the beauty of Bella basking in the early sunshine. We shared the morning paper. It tickled my heart to see her delight in the comic pages. Bella was my dream come true.

In the meantime, the distaste between Mummy and me had grown palpable. Sometimes, she would startle me with her seemingly magical appearances. She studied me with her evil, jaundiced eyes. Mummy seemed to know me better than anyone, and I hated her for it. She used her knowledge of my likes and dislikes to torture me mentally. I would find my glasses broken, my favorite sweater ripped, the sports pages of the Sunday paper shredded.

After almost two years of living in fear of her next move, I decided I had to do something about Mummy. I prepared all our meals, always using fresh meats and vegetables. The finicky senior's favorite was my wild poached salmon with hollandaise sauce.

That night, I prepared it as I usually did. Mummy hovered nearby inhaling the delectable smells. I smiled at her, unaware of my mistake. I turned back to the stove, without seeing the distrust on her aging, pallid face. When I looked again, she was gone. Quickly, I reached for the can of rat poison from under the sink where I had stashed it earlier and sprinkled it generously on Mummy's portion.

I carried the plates to the dining room where Bella sat in her usual spot. The old one was nowhere in sight. As I gently placed Bella's plate in front of her, she looked lovingly at me. I set my plate at the head of the table, careful to put Mummy's plate in her regular spot. "I'll look for Mummy," I said to Bella. "I don't want her food to get cold."

I went to the third floor to check Mummy's room. She wasn't there. On her windowsill, I noticed the gold cufflink that I had been missing.

"You won't be stealing my things anymore," I muttered under my breath.

I checked the laundry room on the way downstairs. It was empty as well. My dress shirt was on the floor, with a dark stain.

"You've got it coming," I said louder than I had intended.

When I returned to the dining room, there was Mummy. She picked her head up and licked the creamy salmon from her lips. Satisfaction melted from my face when I realized that Mummy was eating from Bella's plate. Sheer panic turned in my stomach when I saw Bella put the last piece of fish in her mouth from Mummy's dish. "Noo," I cried.

The heartless matriarch continued to eat as Bella went into convulsions and died in front of my eyes. I scooped up Bella's lifeless body in my arms and sobbed into her warm neck. Through watery eyes, I watched Mummy lick her plate and slowly leave the room.

I dug the hole under the bird feeder. Kneeling beside her, I stroked Bella's soft head one last time, before I wrapped her body in the Sunday comics. Placing Bella's pink collar and her favorite stuffed mouse on top of her, I filled in the hole. Yellow eyes looked down at me from the third floor. Mummy sat on the windowsill contentedly lapping her paws.

BONE OF CONTENTION

Kathy Chencharik

The shop whistle blew at midnight. Outside, the skeleton crew arose for their graveyard shift.

"What's keeping those lazybones?" Fred, the foreman, muttered as he opened the door and peered outside.

In the moonlit yard, he noticed eight skeletons instead of the usual seven. "What are you hanging around for?" he shouted. "Get in here and get to work!"

"I've got a bone to pick with you, Fred," the newcomer said as it lifted its carpals and wiggled one of his phalanges.

Fred stormed out of the shop, past the row of workers. He stopped, coming face to skull with the one who had spoken. "Who are you, a new recruit?"

"No. I'm the new union leader, Fred. I hear you pay bare bones. Not even the minimum wage."

"You a troublemaker?" Fred shouted as he stared into empty eye sockets. "And how do you know my name?"

"Don't you recognize me, Fred? We used to work together."

A bead of sweat broke out across Fred's brow, and the hairs on the nape of his neck stood on end. "Jimmy?" Fred gulped. "Is that you?"

The skeleton nodded its skull. "You know you didn't have to resort to murder to get my job."

Jimmy rattled his bones. The other skeletons gathered together and lifted Fred into the air, tossing him into a shallow grave.

"Cheer up, Fred." Jimmy chuckled as he looked down and shoveled the first load of dirt over him. "We'll soon be working together again."

GNOME FOR THE HOLIDAYS

Diane Kane

I look like a crazy woman, beating the inside of the frozen windshield of my rundown Volkswagen bug. I choke on the exhaust fumes seeping into the car from the broken tailpipe. I hadn't noticed the toxic smell in the hour-and-forty-three-minute trip to spend Christmas with my above average family. I spent the whole ride stressing about my lack of accomplishments since my last visit to Aunt Sheila's house on Thanksgiving.

In the parking lot of the Speedy Mart on the corner of Main and Primrose Drive, just down the hill from my aunt's stately Victorian house, with my window half-way down, I suck on the last cigarette to touch my lips for the rest of the afternoon. Cursing, I wonder why I agreed to spend Christmas with my eccentric aunt, her overachieving children, and their devil offspring—not to mention the gnome!

Forget, about the gnome! I reprimand myself while I toss the stub of my cigarette out the window and blow smoke into the icy breeze. *He's already cost you hundreds of dollars in therapy.*

The therapist claims I have distrust issues. She tells me that I desire the company of an imaginary male role model.

Grasping the old window handle with two hands, I struggle to crank up the frosty glass. With a loud bang, the window slips the track and tilts at a 30-degree angle two inches from the top. Grinding my teeth, I drive up the hill peering through a thin film of ice, while the sub-zero wind blows through my hair.

My nose twitches in the cold breeze, reminding me again of the annoying little gnome. I chew on my lip, considering how real he looked at Thanksgiving when he put his chubby hands on his portly hips and told me dirty little secrets about my not-so-perfect family.

A laugh escapes my lips when I remember how one of my twin nieces held Gnome up by his little red boots. He was so happy that I saved him.

I curse as I almost drive by Aunt Sheila's house. I swing my decrepit VW into the driveway and park next to Cousin William's shiny new Lexus SUV. I jam a shoulder into my sticky door, cringing as it almost hits William's expensive vehicle. The rickety car door slams shut, causing the window to fall with a sickening crack.

As I shuffle my way up the winding brick walkway toward Aunt Sheila's grand Victorian home, goosebumps rise on my arms. I spy the pointy red cap of my nemesis from halfway down the path.

"So, you're still here," I say as I approach him. "At least they let *me* in the house."

I reach out to grasp the railing before mounting the wooden stairs to the sprawling porch. The toe of my shoe catches on the first step. Propelled forward, I land in a heap on the cold stairs. My eyes roll around in my head chasing stars, and I hear buzzing in my ears. Through blurred eyes, I see the gnome's whiskers twitching.

"It's not funny!"

"Aunt Becky!" My spooky twin nieces Makayla and Michaela appear at the top of the steps with blank looks on their mirrored faces. I can't even tell which one spoke. Makes no difference; I can't tell them apart. "We've been waiting for you! Our parents won't let us open our presents without you."

"Rebecca!" Aunt Sheila rushes out the front door onto the porch. "Why on earth are you hanging about out here?" She grabs my arm and pulls me up the steps.

"I was talking to the twins."

"Walking in the wind?" Aunt Sheila questions.

"No, twins…"

"Gin?" Aunt Sheila asks. "We have some in the liquor cabinet. Drinks before noon? You *are* your father's daughter, Rebecca."

"Get in the house, girls!" she tells the twins and shuts the massive oak door solidly behind us.

The entry hall overflows with poinsettias. I inhale the smell of the fresh pine garland that wraps the curved staircase to the second floor. Christmas carols float in the air, and I get a warm feeling inside. Since my parents passed away, Aunt Sheila and her brood are the only blood relatives I have left. Several rungs separate us on the social ladder, but we are family after all.

My excessively handsome cousin William greets me in his three-piece Italian suit, "Becky," he pauses. "New hairdo?"

"Yes." I sweep my wind-blown locks over my shoulder.

"It's *you*." His eyes twitch. William never could lie well.

"Becky." My cousin Catherine waltzes into the room and embraces me. "What is that scent you're wearing?"

"It's a new German cologne." Called VW exhaust, I fail to add.

"William," Aunt Sheila says. "Rebecca needs a gin and tonic. Come to think of it, so do I."

We retire to the sitting room, where William's flaunty model wife and Catherine's two-timing husband are sitting just a little too close. William hands me a glass, and I relax with the burn of gin warming my insides and numbing my mind. Getting comfortable in the overstuffed chair, I feel something hard and pointy jab into my posterior. Reaching in between the cushions I suck in my breath as my hand touches the unmistakable contours of a chubby gnome. I jump from my chair with a squeal.

"Why, Rebecca," Aunt Shelia slurs with the voice of someone who cannot hold her liquor. "What on earth has gotten into you? You look like you've been goosed." Her laughter bubbles.

My face flushes in numerous shades of red. Young Willy runs into the room shrieking, with the twins chasing behind him. Young Willy dives into my chair while the twins tickle him.

“There’s something stuck in this cushion,” one of the twins says, pulling out the little figure. “It’s our gnome.” She looks at me with furrowed eyebrows.

I grab the statue from her grimy hands and feel the gnome trembling.

“Rebecca,” Aunt Shelia says. “You seem to have an obsession with our garden gnome.”

My cousins, William and Catherine, and both their significant others consider me curiously.

I straighten my shoulders and take a deep breath. “I want to tell the children a Christmas story,” I improvise. “The gnome is part of the story.” I place the whiskered statue on the mantle for safety.

The twins look at me with suspicion as my mind races with possibilities.

“Sit down, children,” Catherine instructs them. “Let Auntie Becky tell you the gnome story.” The children sit cross-legged in front of the fireplace. Every eye in the room is upon me.

"Well, uh," I stammer. "Once upon a time…" Behind my attentive audience, the gnome limbers up, stretching his arms over his head and shaking his hips. "Santa's list of children was getting sooo long that he needed…Help!" I yell the last word as the gnome nearly falls off the mantel while doing jumping jacks.

He hangs on by one chubby hand and swings his leg over the edge. I breathe a sigh of relief as he pulls himself back onto the shelf.

"Soo… Santa decided to ask all the garden gnomes to help him." I give the gnome my sternest look. "And the gnomes agreed."

"What do the gnomes do for Santa, Auntie Becky?" Makayla or Michaela asked.

"That's a great question, Michyala." I slur the two names together with the ease that a good gin provides. "The gnomes listen for everyone's Christmas wishes, and they magically relate them to Santa."

The gnome sticks his thumbs in his ears and waves his fingers at me while jutting out his tongue. I shake my head and smile at the foolish imp, in spite of myself.

"So always be nice to your gnome, and maybe he will be nice to you," I end emphatically.

We proceed to open all our presents, and to my great relief, everyone gets their wishes. My gnome story holds true. The gnome blows on his curled fingers and rubs them on his vest.

I table the gin and finish the afternoon with eggnog (unspiked). After dessert, I pluck the gnome from his high perch on the mantel and return him to his post in the garden by the front steps.

"Thanks for telling that terrific story about my magical powers," he whispers. "I have a feeling I'm going to be treated a little better around here."

"How did you get yourself into my chair, anyway?" I ask.

"I hopped into your coat pocket when you were sprawled out on the steps," he snickers.

I shake my head and smile. "See if you can stay out of trouble," I tell him as I set him securely on the ground.

His whiskers part and he flashes a toothy grin before clasping his arms behind his back. I exhale a startled gasp as my whimsical friend turns to stone before my astonished eyes.

"Wait until I tell my therapist this one."

TOO MANY COOKS

Sharon A. Harmon

While spending four years in the Swiss Alps under the tutelage of his uncle Michael, a gourmet cook, Pierre had become a master chef as well as an avid skier.

"You spend too much time womanizing. Your social life should begin only after you master my secret techniques for wonderful cuisine," his uncle's voice thundered in his memory.

Nevertheless, he had still found time to perfect the soufflé and to master decadent desserts. Pierre created such pieces of art that some were photographed in *Bon Appétit* magazine, much to his uncle's chagrin.

Pierre finally escaped from under his uncle's heavy hand and now lived at the Woodstock Inn in Vermont. It was luck that brought him to the mountainous resort as an assistant cook. He would have been euphoric if not for the appearance of his uncle Michael. Not wanting his nephew to get the upper hand, Uncle Michael made his way to Vermont in hot pursuit of Pierre and the job of head cook with his phony French accent.

Month after month Uncle Michael continued to scold, reprimand, and belittle Pierre. "You are too heavy with your cream sauces, and your use of herbs is too understated," he ranted. Day in and day out, Pierre took his uncle's verbal abuse as he violently chopped vegetables, causing his signature cakes to fall.

Valentine's Day should have been Pierre's sweet revenge. Mysteriously, his uncle had been out of work for almost a week. Pierre had filled in for him, basking in the "compliments to the chef" that he received from the diners.

At last, he was getting to show off some of the desserts that had made him famous. Things were going along wonderfully, until an irate guest complained of something in his tiramisu that looked very much like a human tooth.

With a snowstorm imminent, many major roads had already been closed. Pierre stuffed his passport into a knife holder around his waist. Time was of the essence, and Pierre's skiing skills came into great use as he skied downhill still dressed in his cook's attire trying to beat the storm.

DNR

Kathy Chencharik

"A penny for your thoughts." Seventy-year-old Phyllis Corkscrew glanced up into the mirror. She watched as her hairdresser's reflection took out a blow-dryer.

"I was thinking about my doctor's appointment tomorrow at Universal Hospital in Webster," she said. "I hate the drive. It's boring."

"Why not ask Kim to go and keep you company? She's usually free."

"That's not a bad idea. I think I'll give her a call when I get home."

***

At 8 a.m. the next morning, Phyllis's phone rang. She picked it up on the third ring.

"Phyllis, this is Jake. Your sister Coral wasn't feeling well, so I brought her to the emergency room last night. They transferred her to Universal Hospital in Webster."

"Is she okay?"

"Last I heard, she might need surgery."

"I have an appointment there today. I'll stop in to see Coral."

“She’s in room 529.”

“Thanks. I’ll call Stan and Henrietta. I believe Henrietta has an appointment there today as well. Maybe they’ll stop in to see her, too.”

“That would be great.”

“Okay, I’ll leave earlier than planned, but first I have to make another call.”

“Good morning, this is Phyllis,” she said when Kim answered. “When it rains it pours. My sister Coral ended up at Universal Hospital. I’m going in to see her before and after my appointment. I know you said you’d go with me, so if you don’t want to go, I’d understand.”

“What time are we leaving?”

“In thirty minutes.”

“I’ll be ready.”

When they arrived at the hospital, Phyllis dropped her car off at valet parking. They walked a short distance along a sidewalk before entering the hospital.

“Wow,” Kim said, glancing around. “This place is enormous.”

“I know. Coral’s on the fifth floor. The elevators are over there.” Phyllis pointed.

"Elevators?" Kim asked in alarm. "I don't do elevators. I'll take the stairs and meet you there. Room 529 you said?"

"Yes, and you'll probably beat me," Phyllis said with a laugh.

Kim left Phyllis waiting for an elevator and headed for the door to the stairs. By the time she reached the fifth-floor landing, she was huffing and puffing. I'm getting too old for this, Kim thought. Two green doors with a couple of small windows were on either side of the landing. Kim walked over to the door on the left. She peered in through a window, grabbed the handle and pulled. The door was locked. She crossed over to the door on the right. It was locked as well.

"*What the. . .?*" Kim wondered. She walked down a flight of stairs to the fourth floor, and once again, she noticed two doors on either side. Walking over to one, she pulled the handle, and the door opened. Kim stepped into the hallway and spotted two nurses nearby. "Excuse me," she said, "but I'm trying to get to the fifth floor, and the doors are locked."

"Oh," one of the nurses replied. "You have to ring the buzzer. Someone will let you in."

"Buzzer?" Kim asked in surprise.

"Yes, ring the buzzer."

Once again, Kim trudged up to the fifth floor. She looked at the door on the left. No buzzer. She walked to the door on the right. No buzzer. However, she did spot someone through one of the small windows. Kim rapped on the glass. A nurse came over to the window and said, "You can't come in. The doors are locked."

"I know that. But I'm trying to get to room 529."

"This is the pediatric ward. We keep the doors locked. You can't come in."

Kim shrugged her shoulders, turned, and once more started down the stairs. When she reached the third-floor landing, she heard a noise from above. She glanced up and saw a young man dressed in a white lab coat descending the stairs. *Oh, great*, Kim thought, *they're coming to take me away, ha ha.*

As the young man was about to pass her on the landing, she said, "Excuse me, but can you tell me how to get to room 529? The doors up there were locked."

"Yes, I know," he said. "You need to take the other set of stairs near the elevators."

“Other set?” Kim asked before she passed out.

Wondering what was keeping Kim, Phyllis stopped by the fifth-floor nurse’s station. As she was about to ask if anyone had seen her friend, she heard a voice announce over the intercom, “Code Blue, third-floor landing.”

Phyllis had an uneasy feeling. She followed a nurse to the elevator and went down to the third floor. When they arrived, Phyllis saw a doctor leaning over a woman’s body. Not any woman’s body, but her friend Kim’s. She recognized the pink socks and Dr. Scholl’s. The doctor loosened Kim’s blouse, then stood up.

“What are you doing?” Phyllis shouted. “That’s my friend. Get down there and do some CPR or something!”

“I can’t,” he said, looking at Phyllis. “The woman has DNR tattooed across her chest. That means do not resuscitate.”

“I know what it means, Einstein, but the DNR on her chest happens to stand for Dean Nicholas Radford, her first love. She’s had that tattoo since high school. So, start pumping!”

Kim awoke in a hospital bed. She glanced around the room and saw Coral in the next bed. Jake, Stan, Henrietta, and Phyllis were sitting beside her.

"Did I finally make it to the fifth floor?"

"Yes," Phyllis said, walking over and picking up her friend's hand.

"What happened? How'd I end up here?"

"You fainted. At first, everyone thought you'd had a heart attack. The doctor almost didn't do CPR because of David Nicholas Radford."

"Oh, yeah," Kim said with a laugh. "The DNR tattoo you wanted me to get rid of."

"At your age, you should have it removed. If it had been a heart attack and I hadn't been there to explain, you could have died. But luckily you fainted from dehydration. No need for CPR. They said you could leave once you woke up."

Kim nodded. She looked over at Coral and waved.

Coral smiled and waved back.

"How's she doing?" Kim asked.

"She just came back a little while ago from minor surgery."

"That's good," Kim said as she got out of bed. "What about your appointment?"

"All done. I went while you were out of it. Now, go get dressed so we can go home."

"Okay." Kim picked up her clothes and headed for the bathroom. "But I think I'll stick with you and use the elevators this time. Those stairs are killers."

MUD WRESTLING IN THE GARDEN

Phyllis Cochran

Torrential downpours swept through the town of Winchendon for a week and a half, leaving the ground soggy. Driving home from a writers' luncheon, Deidre noticed the sun peeking out.

Arriving home, she hurried into the house. "I'm heading for the garden to pick the vegetables," she told her husband. "The squash and cucumbers must be huge."

"You're going to do that now?" Brad asked, surprised. "It will be too muddy."

"I'll be careful where I step."

Deidre quickly changed into her duck boots but left her dressy white slacks and jacket on.

The grass seemed a bit squishy, as she walked the distance toward the back garden. Oversized squash and cucumbers sprawled out from beneath the vines onto the lawn. Deidre stretched over the first row and picked a couple of summer squash. When she couldn't reach those on the other side, she cautiously climbed over the plant.

The ground is a bit mushy, but not bad; another step or two to grab the cucumbers. Still okay.

The peppers grew in the next row, and she moved closer with no problem. *Guess it wasn't that wet*, she mused.

When she finished picking the peppers, Deidre glanced toward the lawn from where she had come. She decided not to cross back the same way. The end of the garden was about four feet from the grass, and no plants grew in the area, so she took a step in that direction. Mud gobbled up her right foot. She heard a sucking sound as her duck boot and leg submerged about 9 inches into what seemed like quicksand.

Now I'm in trouble.

Deidre tried to free her foot, struggling to move forward or backward to no avail. She certainly couldn't remain like this for the rest of the afternoon.

Maybe if I step across to the right with my left foot, there will be firmer ground.

Deidre's left foot also quickly disappeared as the sludge tightened its grip. Feeling wobbly, with legs crossed and mud clinging to her calves, she fell sideways.

Too late to worry about getting my white clothes dirty. Clumps of brown muck clung to her garments.

Deidre needed to get to her feet, a maneuver that might have gone smoothly if she'd been a child. Her aging legs, however, had different ideas.

Where are the neighbors now when I need help? They usually see everything, but no one is in sight this afternoon. Brad is probably dozing in his chair.

With the windows closed, shouting for help wasn't an option.

Guess it's up to me to find a way to win this battle. Here I go, she mused, plunging both hands deliberately into the mud, feeling for a shelf of solid ground to lean on.

Eventually, she made contact. Hunched over, Deidre pushed upward, freeing one foot from a duck boot. She continued, using various contortions with her legs, feet, hands, and arms until her legs uncrossed.

Suddenly she broke loose and lurched upward onto both feet. Balancing on one foot, Deidre fumbled around beneath the sloppy surface to retrieve one duck boot and tossed it toward the lawn. Maneuvering awkwardly forward, she sloshed through the mud in a straight line, while sinking down with each step, and made it to the grass. Gobs of goop slid off her outfit.

Leaving behind a missing boot and bag of vegetables, Deidre plodded in nylon stocking feet to the outside faucet. After hosing herself from top to bottom, she climbed the back stairs dripping brown water all the way.

Entering the house, she could hear the television in the living room—not a sound from Brad. He was probably reclining dry and calm. Still frazzled, Deidre headed for a warm shower, she wasn't ready to hear him say I told you so.

Maybe later, when she was relaxed, she could tell him about her first attempt at mud wrestling. Perhaps then she would laugh, but not at that moment.

KILT IN ACTION

Kathy Chencharik

Judge Fox loosened the collar of his long black robe. He peered down from his bench at the five men standing before him, all dressed in skirts.

"Officer Grant, please approach the bench," the judge said. He leaned down and whispered into the arresting officer's ear, "I thought this was a disorderly conduct case. Why are these cross-dressers here?"

"They're not cross-dressers, your honor," the officer whispered back. "They're Scottish, and those are kilts they're wearing."

The judge turned to the defendants and said, "You've been charged with disorderly conduct. How do you plead?"

"Not guilty, your honor," Angus MacDuff replied in his gruff accent as he stepped forward. "You see, our dear friend, Ian Kirkpatrick, recently moved here from Scotland. He had told us about a drive-thru car wash back home that he had loved. Alas, he recently died of a heart attack. As we were on our way to the cemetery, we spotted a sign for a car wash and decided to send him through one last time as we played our bagpipes in tribute." He handed a picture of them at the car wash to the judge.

"This proves you were there," Judge Fox said as he looked at the picture. "How can that possibly help your case?"

"If you'd please read the sign in the picture your honor."

"Full-service car wash," the judge read aloud.

"Aye. Where else but in America can you hold a memorial service at a car wash?"

"Not guilty," the judge ruled with a smile. He brought his gavel down. "Next case?"

TRICK OR TREAT?

Diane Kane

After years of being a starving writer, I recently published an incredibly popular murder mystery series *Murder Over Fifty-Five*. Being a famous author is everything I ever dreamt it would be—book signings, fan clubs, fame, and fortune—the problem is I didn't actually write it all.

It started innocently one late night just over a year ago. I sat in front of my computer screen with fingers placed on the keyboard. I told myself that if I was ever going to be published I needed to be able to write a mainstream murder mystery with humor. Enough of my gloom-and-doom tales; this time I was going to write funny. The problem is, I'm not funny. I'm sulky and serious, sensitive and sullen—which equals gloom and doom. I was determined not to give up this time. Thirty minutes passed, my eyes started to blur and my fingers cramped. That's when I first heard her voice.

"Stop sitting there like a dumbass and start typing," she said, plain as day.

"What?" I jumped and looked around my empty apartment.

"Exactly what I tell you, that's what!"

While I was shaking my head trying to clear the cobwebs that were apparently causing me to hallucinate, my fingers started to type. I stared in amazement as my usual forty-word-a-minute fingers were flying across the keys doing at least a hundred. Intently, I watched the screen as words formed sentences that made sense, not just gobbledygook. I marveled that the sentences flowed into paragraphs that told a story. It was engaging, interesting and—strangest of all—it was funny.

"Stop shaking your head and pay attention!" she shouted.

"Who the heck are you?"

"I'm Eileen, you numbskull. Don't you see my name in the story you're writing?"

"I'm writing…?"

"Well, technically you *are* hitting the keys. I can't type since I'm a figment of your imagination."

"But—you're talking to me."

"Yes, yes, I'm talking to you. Someone has to give you a push if you ever want to be published. And I have a great story to tell. So let's get to it."

***

A year later, I'd finished my second in the series and was working on my third highly anticipated book. I had no idea what Eileen was going to tell me to write. One thing I was sure of: she would tell me. I was also sure it would be good…and it would be funny.

It was late October, and I had just returned from a grueling book tour of eight states, twenty-four bookstores, and one state fair. I was exhausted, and I refused to communicate with Eileen until I'd gotten some rest. I sat in my comfy recliner and eased it back when I heard a ruckus outside my front door.

Struggling to get out of my chair, I hurried across the living room in my stocking feet, clumsily sliding to the door. Grabbing the doorknob and looking out the side window, I couldn't believe what I was seeing.

I rubbed both my tired eyes and peered out a second time only to see the same thing. It was Eileen…and not just one of her. On my front step, down my stairs, winding around my walkway, all the way to the street, there were images of Eileen as far as the eye could see.

"Open the door, you idiot. Can't you see they want to come in?" said the voice in my head.

"But—but—you're in my head. And there is only supposed to be one of you."

"You can never have too much of a good thing," she laughed.

"One of you is more than enough!"

"Diane, sometimes I get the feeling you don't appreciate me. Where exactly would you be without me?"

"At this moment, I would be resting comfortably in my recliner."

The knocking persisted at the front door.

"Diane," Eileen said with impatience. "You have company."

"I don't want company! Leave me alone!"

Just like that, she was gone. I peeked out the side window of the front door. The wind blew fallen leaves across my empty walkway; a single streetlight shone on a deserted road. In my barren living room, the ticking clock on the wall was the only sound that broke the eerie silence.

"Eileen?" I whispered. "Eileen!"

My eyes scanned the room and my sights landed on the computer. I hurried over and fired it up. Eileen couldn't stay away if I sat at the keyboard. She would have to put in her two cents.

I sat with my fingers poised on ASDF—JKL; I waited and waited.

"Eileen!" I yelled. "Where are you?" I walked over to my recliner and slumped into it. "I'm sorry," I sobbed. "I can't do this without you."

"You got that right," I heard a familiar voice say.

"Eileen!" I turned toward the voice only to find it was Eileen in flesh and blood.

I would have thrown my arms around her if I wasn't worried that she would disappear.

"Here, put these on," she said as she threw a shirt, pants, and hat at me.

Looking them over, I realized she had handed me a postal uniform.

"You want me to dress up like my book character Clare, the mail lady?"

"That's the idea, honey."

"But why?"

"You didn't like it when I brought the Halloween party to you, so we're going to the party.

You certainly can't go looking like a..." she said, looking me over. "…psychotic author."

"So I'm going as a character in a psychotic author's book?"

"Yes," Eileen laughed. "And you are going with a figment of your imagination!"

"I *am* psychotic," I said, shaking my head.

***

"Diane! Wake up; you're having a nightmare!"

I could hear a voice yelling at me from what seemed a great distance. I opened my eyes to find my neighbors Susan and Debra standing right in front of me. I jumped out of my recliner as though I'd been shot from a cannon.

"What happened?" I asked breathlessly.

"We heard you screaming from our apartment and came running over," Debra said.

"Your door was unlocked, so we came in to see if you were all right," Susan continued. "We had a time trying to wake you up. You must have been having one crazy dream."

I looked around the room. Eileen was nowhere in sight. Still dressed in the clothes I'd come home in, with no hint of a postal uniform. I took a deep breath and exhaled.

"I must have fallen asleep in my recliner," I said, relieved. "My dream seemed so real."

"What was it about?" asked Debra.

"I dreamt my muse Eileen was right here in my apartment. She wanted me to go to a Halloween party, and she had me dress up like my character Clare, the mail lady." I paused. "And there was a murder!"

"Sounds like you have the next chapter for your upcoming book." Debra smiled.

"Oh, it looks like you've already been working on it," Susan said excitedly, pointing toward the words on my computer screen.

My heart leaped. "I never know what's going to appear on my computer screen," I said. "One thing I know for sure—it will be funny."

Number One

B.F. PARK

Kathy Chencharik

Sentenced to die at midnight, serial killer Freddie Winslow was about to be strapped into the electric chair when the power went out. Thunder rattled the windows and lightning lit up the room as he was hustled out, flanked by his priest and executioner.

"Dead man walking," a prisoner called out from the dark.

"Echo man talking," Freddie replied. "You said that the first time I walked by. I won't fry tonight. They had to cut me loose because they ran out of juice."

"What time is it?" the executioner asked the priest as they rounded a corner.

"Eleven forty-five. God forgive us. We still have fifteen minutes."

"We'll make it," the executioner said as he grabbed an umbrella and they quickly headed outside.

"Hey!" Freddie shouted above a clap of thunder. "Where are you taking me?"

"To B.F. Park," the executioner replied.

They all hurried out into the middle of an open field and stopped. Gazing up at the lightning-riddled sky, the executioner opened the umbrella, removed the rubber handle, and handed it to Freddie.

“Thanks,” he said as he took it. “So, what does the B.F. stand for?”

Suddenly, at midnight, a bolt of lightning struck the umbrella, killing Freddie instantly.

The executioner announced the time of death, then looking down at Freddie’s smoldering body he said, “Benjamin Franklin.”

THE CHICKEN SALAD HIT THE FAN

Diane Kane

I slumped at the kitchen table in my mother's house with the last remains of coffee cold in my cup. I had stopped by with a cup for each of us, and her favorite honey-dipped donut. At least it was her favorite until today.

"Oh honey, I can't tolerate all the sugar on that donut. And that coffee would keep me up all night."

That's funny, I thought, *it's not keeping me awake at all.*

I rubbed my eyes as my mother proceeded to tell me once again about her swollen ankles. I wondered how many more ways she could describe them as I drifted off to a more peaceful place.

"Diane!" she shouted. "Are you listening to me?"

My drooping head jerked up. "I'm just exhausted from working all day," I said. "I better get home."

"Oh, yes, I used to be tired when I worked, slept like a log. Now I'm up all night between peeing and letting the cats in and out. No need for sleep, I'll sleep when I'm dead. You know, these swollen ankles could be the death of me. My friend Agnes, she had swollen ankles went straight to her heart. Diane, are you listening to me?"

When she paused for a breath, I hurried to the door. "I'll call you tomorrow," I promised.

I made it to my car, started it up, and pulled out of the driveway before she could run out and tell me just one more thing. Driving down the road, I looked over at the passenger seat and saw the container of chicken salad that I'd meant to give her. I couldn't bring myself to go back. I had a great idea.

I'll stop by the senior living complex on Cross Street and give it to Uncle Otto. I go right by there on my way home.

I parked in the back parking lot near the door to his one-room apartment. No need to buzz in, everyone knew me there. One of the adorable elderly women opened the door. I had just come around the corner to Uncle Otto's hallway when he zipped my way on his three-wheel electric handicapped scooter. He'd voluntarily given up his car three years ago, and this was the third scooter he'd had in as many years.

"Hey, Uncle Otto, new scooter?"

"Diane! Good to see you. I'm just breaking this scooter in. I got it up to 35 mph yesterday; hoping to break the big four'O today!"

"Better watch you don't break your neck. You still got the bruises from your last crash."

"Backlash? I don't have none of that."

Uncle Otto was ninety-three and entirely unaware that he was hard of hearing.

"Where you headed?" I yelled.

"Going to get my ears lowered." He grinned. "And take this stool sample to the doctor's office."

"Okay…well, I brought you some chicken salad."

"Thanks, I could use some fricken salad. If I'd had that this morning maybe I wouldn't have had such a hard time getting this stool sample."

"Chicken, Uncle Otto," I yelled.

"Who are you calling a chicken? You know I'm a veteran, Diane."

"Not you, the salad."

"Oh, well, I'm not prejudiced. I'll eat it whatever it is," he said. "Just put it in my icebox; the door is unlocked. I have to get this stool sample to the doctor before it turns bad."

Briefly wondering if a stool sample could go bad, I realized it wasn't something I wanted to ponder.

I looked around with an odd feeling that someone had been eavesdropping on our conversation. Laughing to myself, I remembered that none of the residents in the building could hear our conversation without turning their hearing aids all the way up.

Uncle Otto scraped the walls with his new scooter as he made his way down the hall. Opening the door to his apartment, the smell of pine trees and gladiolas assaulted my nasal passages. Glancing toward the bathroom, I identified the origin of both. On his sink was a sample-size plastic bottle of Brut Cologne and the colorful metal Glade bathroom spray can.

There was plenty of room in his refrigerator. He had a small container of milk, a dried-up black banana, and an unidentifiable piece of meat.

I put the container of chicken salad next to the milk. I left happy that Uncle Otto would have a healthy snack when he returned from his errands.

***

The next day when I got home from work, I heard my phone ringing when I walked in the door.

"How dare you tell me you were so tired yesterday? You weren't too tired to take your delicious chicken salad to Uncle Otto."

"Hello, Mom." I tried to interrupt without success.

"He says your chicken salad is better than mine. Mine is messy, he claims, and yours is just right. Well, he'll never get any more of my chicken salad, I can tell you that." Click.

I had just hung up the phone and started to take my coat off when the phone rang again.

"Diane!" Uncle Otto shouted.

"Hi, Uncle Otto," I shouted back.

"Oh, Diane, I made a big mess of things with the chicken salad."

"What happened, Uncle Otto?"

"Your mother asked me over for lunch today. She had made chicken salad, and it was good, don't get me wrong. Not as good as yours, but I wasn't going to tell her that." He took a deep breath and continued.

"She kept asking me if yours was better. I told her I liked hers, but yours had just the right amount of mayonnaise. But she wouldn't let it go, Diane; she kept after me about hers having too much and was it messy.

She was smiling, so I thought we were joking around." He moaned.

"I told her how hers squirted out the sides of the bread and got all over my hands but yours didn't. That's when I knew by the look on her face that we weren't joking anymore."

"It's all right Uncle Otto," I assured him.

"Oh, Diane, she is so mad. What am I going to do? I wouldn't even have told her you brought me the chicken salad…"

"Wait a minute; you didn't tell her?"

"No, I thought you did."

"Hmm, she was snooping on us."

"Don't be calling your mother pooping names, Diane. She's a good woman. She means well; she can just be a little jealous at times."

"I know. Don't worry, Uncle Otto. It will blow over."

***

When I went to visit my mother the next day, the weather had changed and so had the conversation. Her swollen ankles had deflated, and now her shoulders were acting up.

"This bursitis is killing me. My tendons and muscles are all stiff and inflamed. It could be an autoimmune disorder. My friend Margaret had this very same thing, and it turned into the gout. You know people can die of the gout; I've heard it's happened. Diane, are you listening to me? You could get this, you know; it's in your genes."

I never heard the words chicken salad again. But just in case, while my mother continued to ramble on about the facts of bursitis and the poor state of my gene pool, I made a few mental notes about the principles of giving chicken salad.

First, never tell my mother I'm tired and going home then take chicken salad to Uncle Otto. She is not too old to jump in her car and follow me.

Second, when giving chicken salad, give to both her and Uncle Otto at the same time so as to avoid any appearance of favoritism.

Last and most important, never make chicken salad that tastes better than my mother's does.

Come to think of it, scratch all that.

NEVER make chicken salad again.

FOWL LANGUAGE

Kathy Chencharik

Maggie came out of the store with change. She fed the parking meter before returning to the passenger's seat to wait for Will.

"Know anything about a murder of crows?" hissed a voice from the backseat. Maggie jumped.

It must be Will, she thought. *He's playing a trick on me. Two can play this game.*

She laughed and said, "Somebody killed a bunch of crows?" Maggie started to turn in her seat.

"Don't turn around or I'll peck your eyes out!" came another hiss. "Your knowledge of birds is obviously limited."

Maggie stiffened and faced front, realizing it wasn't Will after all. "Who . . .who . . .who are you?"

"I'm not an owl. Visit the Boston Public Gardens lately? I heard you made a swan dive and how shall I put this? Ab-duck-ted something?"

"Think I'll sing like a canary?" Maggie asked. "You must be cuckoo."

"Wrong again."

The driver's side door opened and Will got in. "We made a bundle on that Boston bird," he said, tossing money into her lap.

"Shut up!" Maggie motioned toward the back seat.

Will turned. "Hey, where'd the mute come from?"

"Mute?" Maggie said with a laugh. "He's anything but. Do you recognize him?"

"Recognize him?" Will said, looking at her askance. "They all look the same to me. Bet Tony will buy this one too."

In confusion, Maggie turned and gazed into the beady black eyes of a swan. She screamed.

All of a sudden, police surrounded their car. "Get that transmitter off the mute swan's neck," the captain said. "We've got what we needed."

MATCHING TUX

Diane Kane

Suzanne's mood matched the gloomy day. Although her husband had passed away five years ago, she couldn't seem to move forward.

She was startled from her melancholy by two young co-workers distributing flyers. "The Christmas Ball is just a month away!" they announced. Suzanne gave the paper a cursory glance before slipping it into the wastepaper basket under her desk. She had a lot of work to get done and little desire to think about the ball or anything else.

At 4 p.m., Suzanne grabbed her bag from under the desk and headed home to the well-dressed male that waited patiently for her each day, her black and white cat, Tux.

Tux heard the key turn in the lock and knew his human was home. Suzanne smiled at the elite catitude that matched his tuxedo markings. Arching his back, he leaned in and dragged his body across Suzanne's leg while she scratched his head. He purred in approval, then headed straight for the back door.

"Time to make your rounds?" She watched him scamper out.

Emptying her work bag, Suzanne was surprised to find the flyer for the ball.

"I must have missed the trash and thrown it in my bag." She shook her head at her mistake and tossed the flyer into the recycling bin.

After dinner, she looked out the door. "Tux," she called. The sun had set, and she was concerned. "Tux," she shouted louder.

"Is this the handsome chap you're looking for?" came a voice from the darkness. The porch light cast on the face of a finely aged gentleman with stunning blue eyes and a well-groomed silver goatee. Tux was nestled in his arms, purring with satisfaction.

Suzanne stammered as she searched for her voice. "Oh, yes, that's—"

"Tux," the man finished, "I heard you calling him. I just moved into the house across the field."

"The old Perkins place?"

"So I'm told. I'm not from these parts."

"I can tell." Suzanne smirked. "Do I detect an English accent?"

"Guilty," he laughed. "My son and his family moved to America, and I was quite lonely in England since my wife passed."

"My husband passed also. My daughter wants me to move near her, but I'm afraid to go."

"I understand."

Suzanne was glad for the night to cover her blush. She couldn't remember the last time she had talked with a handsome man. As if reading her mind, he said, "I've not had the privilege of a conversation with a lovely woman in quite some time. I've rather enjoyed it."

"It's getting late," Suzanne said and reached for Tux.

"My name is Colin," he said and gently set the cat into her arms.

"I'm Suzanne."

"It's been delightful to meet you, Suzanne. And you as well, Tux," he said, with a pat on the cat's head.

"Good night, Colin," Suzanne said with a slight catch in her voice.

Every evening Suzanne let Tux out and Colin would bring him home. After a week, Suzanne asked Colin in.

They had just finished tea when there was a commotion in the kitchen. Tux had scattered the recycle papers all over the floor.

"What's got into you, Tux?" Suzanne scolded.

Colin helped to gather the papers, pausing to read one.

"What's so interesting?" Suzanne asked.

"A flyer about your office ball."

"That silly thing. I don't go anymore since…" Suzanne looked down.

"Mmh," Colin said and stuffed the flyer into his pocket.

The next night Suzanne let Tux out and waited for his return in Colin's arms. The usual time passed with no knock on the door. Perhaps Tux preferred Colin's company to hers, and vice versa, she brooded. Finally hearing a scratch, Suzanne opened the door with a smile only to find Tux. He rubbed against her leg, and a note fell from his collar.

Please allow me to escort you to the ball tomorrow night. Colin.

She beamed. *Why not?*

"Yes," she shouted to the night.

"Woohoo," came the reply.

The next night the two males in Suzanne's life stood on her step in matching tuxedos. "Wow," Suzanne exclaimed.

"I wore this at my son's wedding," Colin said. "I didn't think I'd find another chance to sport it."

Tux strutted past them and curled up on the couch. Colin extended his arm. "Your chariot awaits, my lady."

They danced to almost every song, stopping briefly for a cup of punch. "I haven't had this much fun in years." Suzanne's eyes sparkled. Someone bumped into Colin's arm and his drink spattered across his chest. Suzanne grabbed a napkin to blot the stain. "Now you won't match Tux."

Colin took her hand. "I think the real match is the one Tux made between you and me," Colin said and whisked Suzanne across the dance floor.

Number One

THE LINE WENT DEAD

Kathy Chencharik

"See that phone booth?" Sharon asked. She stood on the street corner and nudged her friend Beverly.

"What about it?"

"It reminds me of a book I once read. *Phone Calls From the Dead.*"

"And I suppose that woman standing next to it, talking on a cell phone, is trying to make contact as we speak."

"Exactly. That's Larry Larkin's wife. He was talking to her from that phone booth the night he dropped dead."

"He made it this far?"

"What do you mean?"

"I live five blocks away. Larry left my house after he finished the poisoned tea I gave him. I thought it would have worked sooner. I guess I'll have to make some adjustments."

"Beverly," Sharon said, staring at her friend. "Are you saying you murdered him? The newspaper said it was his heart."

"How could it have been?" Beverly snickered. "He didn't have one. If he did, he would never have conned my mother out of her life savings."

"He's the one who did that?" Sharon asked.

"Yes."

"Then he deserved it."

The phone in the booth rang. Larry's wife picked it up. "Excuse me," she said, glancing over at Sharon and Beverly as she stepped out of the booth, pulling the cord with her. "But there's a call for a Beverly. Would either of you be she?"

Sharon and Beverly glanced at one another, and in unison, they both shouted, "No!" Then they stepped off the curb and hurried across the street.

"You don't think . . ." Sharon started.

"No, of course not," Beverly said as she glanced back at the booth. "I'm not the only woman named Beverly. But I think I would like to borrow that book."

GNOME AGAIN

Diane Kane

I step with apprehension up the winding brick pathway toward my Aunt Sheila's prestigious Victorian home, stopping dead in my tracks. Ahead of me, beside the porch steps stands the old garden gnome. Gnome and I have an odd relationship. As far as I know, I'm the only person that he talks to, and I wish he wouldn't. There is no end to the trouble he gets me into with my elite and slightly eccentric family.

The weather is warm, and buds are blooming on the trees and bushes, as my allergies can attest. Bending to inspect the gnome closely, I blink in bemusement at the fluffy white ears standing straight up from his red cap and the fuzzy pink nose on his staunch face.

"Ahh choo!" My allergies let loose.

When the dust clears, Gnome is standing with his chubby hands on his hips and a disgusted look on his wet whiskers. With his red cap askew, there isn't a trace of fluffy ears or nose.

I rub my eyes. "I could swear you were just dressed up like a bunny."

"I was before you blew it all away with your gusty turbulence!"

"Allergies," I say apologetically.

"I've been waiting for you," Gnome says.

"Auntie Becky!" My twin nieces, Makayla and Michaela, push their way out the massive front door. "We are waiting for the Easter Bunny."

"Well, let's go inside, so he comes." I stand up and guide them up the stairs.

"Rebecca, I'm so glad you are here," Aunt Sheila greets me breathlessly. She's not wearing her traditional flowered apron. I sniff the air and wonder if my allergies are playing tricks on me. "Aunt Sheila, I don't smell your famous honey ham cooking."

"No, you don't, Rebecca," she sobs into her hands. "The power has gone off, and my holiday ham is sitting stone cold in the pan."

I start to take my coat off, then pull it back on as I feel the chill permeating the air. "How long has the power been off, Aunt Sheila?"

"Since early this morning, it seems," my handsome cousin William briskly answers as he blows through the room with a flashlight in hand. "I've called the electric company. There are no other outages in the area. It has to be something in-house," he says over his shoulder while heading for the cellar stairs.

I wrap my arm around my distraught aunt and guide her into the sitting room, knowing exactly what she needs. William's model wife Stella, usually scantily clad, is curled on the couch like a high-class mummy, with a white cashmere blanket wrapped tight around her skinny body. Catherine and her good-for-nothing husband are arguing by the fireplace.

"Becky," Catherine's voice chimes. "How good to see you!" Her husband Taylor strikes another match and tosses it onto the cold logs. The smell of damp smoke hangs in the air.

Helping Aunt Sheila into her favorite blue wing-backed chair, I head to the liquor cabinet. A good stiff drink will give us more warmth than that fire ever will.

I pour a generous amount of brandy in two snifters and give one to Aunt Sheila. She wraps her hands around the glass and inhales the rich aroma with a weak smile.

"You're a lifesaver, Rebecca." I clink my glass to hers, and we both partake of the liquid heat.

The twins and Young Willy bound into the room breaking the serenity of the moment.

"The Easter Bunny didn't leave any eggs!" Young Willy shrieks.

"And the gnome is missing too!" the twins say in unison.

I feel a tugging inside my pocket. Discreetly slipping my hand in, I feel Gnome's little teeth latch onto my finger. "Ooww!" I scream, attracting everyone's attention.

"Ohhh…" I stutter. "I need to use the powder room." I dash to the bathroom with my brandy in hand.

With the door shut and locked, I set my glass down on the sink and pull Gnome out of my pocket, scowling into his fuzzy face.

"What was the meaning of biting my finger?" "Aah choo!" A tiny puff of wind blows between his whiskers. I wipe my face with disgust. "Sorry," he smirks. "A bit of lint up my nose from being held captive in your dusty pocket."

"Point taken," I concede, setting him on the sink beside my glass while I wash my face and hands.

"I need your help, Rebecca," Gnome says.

"Oh, really?"

"Yes, I need to get rid of a body."

I choke. "Whose body?"

"The Easter rabbit."

I blink in disbelief. "The Easter Bunny is real?"

"He was," Gnome says.

Grabbing my brandy glass, I take a large swallow. "Where's the body?"

Gnome points sheepishly toward the window. "In the garden."

I peer out the window with reluctance and see a big furry mound in the bushes. I cover my eyes, but I can't erase the image. "How did this happen?"

"He chomped into the electric wire."

"Well, that explains why the electricity is out."

Gnome shuffles his feet. "I might have left a bunch of carrots on top of the wire."

"Why would you do that?"

Gnome's face turns as red as his cap. "That rabbit gets all the glory. How hard is it to hide eggs?"

"You're jealous of the Easter Bunny?" I shake my head in disbelief.

"I didn't mean to kill him. I just wanted to give him a good shock. Rebecca, I need your help!"

We both jump at the banging on the bathroom door. "Becky are you all right?" William yells through the door. "Mother said you ran to the bathroom in a tizzy."

"I'm fine, William. Just an upset stomach."

I hear Young Willy crying. "Daddy," he says to William. "Why didn't the Easter Bunny come?"

I scowl at Gnome. "I'll help you this time."

I open the bathroom window and place Gnome on the English Ivy. He scampers down and leaves me to squeeze my size 14 body out of the 16"x 20" opening. Falling with a crash beside the furry rabbit, I stifle a cry. A straw basket lies on its side, and colored eggs are scattered about the ground. Gnome stands beside the bunny biting his fingernails.

"What do we do?" he asks.

I see a slight rise and fall of the bunny's chest. "I don't think he's dead."

The bunny's eyes blink open, and he looks from me to Gnome. His buckteeth stick out, and he lets out a scream.

"Shh," I say trying to calm him and wishing I had more brandy to calm myself.

"You just got a little shock from biting the electric wire," Gnome tries to explain to him.

His eyes dart wildly, and he runs like a scared rabbit into the woods. Gnome and I look at each other.

"What do we do now?" I ask Gnome.

"He left all the eggs." Gnome points out. "If you hide them, I think I can fix the electricity."

There is no time to ask Gnome how he learned to be an electrician, so I get busy hiding eggs. When done, I climb up the English Ivy where Gnome is still hard at work on the wire. Gnome gives me a thumbs up, and I push myself through the bathroom window.

I straighten my disheveled clothes and brush ivy from my hair. Picking up my brandy glass, I down the last of its contents, and stumble out the bathroom door. I shield my eyes to a sudden flash of lights.

My discombobulated family pours out of the sitting room, gawking at the glowing chandelier in the entry hall. The children charge into the house holding colored eggs and talking all at once.

"Auntie Becky!" they screech with glee. "The Easter eggs are everywhere! We need our baskets to collect them." They run to the kitchen to retrieve them and hurry back outside. One of the twins turns around and smiles. "And the gnome is back!"

"That's great, Makayla!" I scratch my head and wonder how I know which twin she is. "It must be magic," I exclaim.

Aunt Sheila grabs her flowered apron off the hook and starts cooking up some magic in the kitchen. The heat blows up from the floor registers and laughter fills the air.

At the end of the day, with a satisfied stomach and a full heart, I hug my not-so-perfect family goodbye and exit out the oak door.

I settle down on the bottom step beside Gnome. “You make a pretty good Easter rabbit, Rebecca.” Gnome smiles.

“Nice work with the electricity,” I say. “How did you fix it?”

“Duct tape,” he chuckles.

“You don’t have to be jealous of the Easter Bunny,” I say and kiss him on the cheek. “You are far smarter than him and a lot cuter too.”

Gnome’s face glows as he puts his arms behind his back and turns to stone once again.

CHAIN REACTION

Kathy Chencharik

Ethel swept her front steps in frustration. She marched across her lawn, broom in hand, dodging cans and papers that littered her yard. Her heart pounded with every boom emanating from the white Tracker parked in front of her house. She approached the vehicle and tapped against the driver's door. The music lowered with the window.

"How many times have I asked you kids to stop tossing litter in my yard?" she asked.

"I give up, old lady, how many?" the young driver said, shrugging his shoulders.

"Too many, Mr. Wise Guy. Next time you do, the police will be doing the asking."

"Look," he said as he pointed to a sign behind him. "That sign says no parking. It's legal to park here."

"Well, it isn't legal to litter," she said as she looked at the sign and got an idea.

"Littering's no big deal," he said. "What are they gonna do, slap my hand?"

His friends laughed. Ethel shook her head and turned to walk away. A can flew out of the window, barely missing her. It landed in her yard. They were still laughing as they drove away.

The next day, the Tracker was back, and there was more litter on her lawn. The radio was louder than ever. Ethel called the police. Then she went out to her shed, picked up a chain she'd bought and dragged it outside. She tied one end to the no parking sign and the other to the Tracker. The radio masked her noise, and she returned to her house.

A cruiser, lights flashing and siren blaring rounded the corner. The Tracker pulled away from the curb, taking the sign with it. Ethel chuckled as she watched the police pull them over. "The boy's right," she said. "Littering's not much of a crime. But stealing city property, now, that's another story!"

MAGIC MOMENTS

Diane Kane

At six years old, Harmony Gleason was a seeker of truth. 'Why?' was Harmony's favorite word, with 'How?' in a close second place.

Santa Claus and the Easter Bunny fascinated Harmony's imagination. She tingled with anticipation of their respective holiday arrivals. Yet, her curious mind couldn't help but question some of their abilities.

"How does Santa fit down this hole with a bag of toys?" she asked her father while sticking her head up the dirty chimney.

"Harmony," her father called out. "Come away from there!" He brushed the ashes from Harmony's clothes as he steered her away from the chimney. "Santa has magic powers, remember?"

Harmony's face twisted while she considered magic powers.

When spring came with Easter preparations, Harmony questioned, "Why does the Easter Bunny bring eggs; shouldn't it be an Easter Chicken?"

"Oh, mm, chickens don't like to travel," her father improvised. "So, they asked a bunny to deliver all the eggs."

Harmony raised one eyebrow in a questioning slant. “But, why…”

“Let’s go get ice cream,” Harmony’s father said, putting a quick end to the Easter Bunny conversation.

Summer meant no fabled characters on the horizon. Harmony’s parents breathed a sigh of relief.

Then one afternoon, Harmony bit into a crisp apple and lost her first tooth. With trepidation, her parents imparted the enchanting story of the fairy who replaced lost teeth with money. Harmony listened to their tale with a dubious expression on her face.

“So, make sure to put your tooth under your pillow tonight,” Harmony’s mother said with an animated smile.

Harmony considered each point of the story as if she was working on a connect-the-dots puzzle. Her eyes narrowed at a particular little dot in the story that seemed out of line.

“Why does the fairy want old teeth?”

“Well, ah,” her father faltered. “Shee, ahh…gives them to babies who don’t have any teeth?”

Harmony’s mother wrinkled her nose. “Well, I don’t know about that, but I’m sure she keeps them in a safe place," she said with an affirmative nod of her head.

That night, Harmony's lips curled with disgust as she examined the tiny white tooth with its pointy root. She placed the hard nugget on her bed, shoving her pillow on top. Then Harmony laid her head down, careful not to disturb the tooth underneath.

Her parents came in to kiss her good night and assured her again that the tooth fairy would take the tooth, leaving money under Harmony's pillow. She heard them giggle as they turned out the light and left the room.

Harmony tossed and turned with anxiety. She was not sure that she wanted to have this strange fairy come into her room. Her parents always told her not to speak to strangers.

"Why is it okay for this creepy fairy to come into my room when I'm sleeping?" Harmony asked her teddy bear.

Teddy stared back at her in bewilderment.

"You're right, Teddy; this is scary." She hugged Teddy tight.

Sometime later, Harmony heard her doorknob rattle. She slid under her covers as her bedroom door slowly opened and someone tiptoed in. Harmony held her breath while a hand slipped under her pillow, retrieving her tiny tooth, and returned to deposit the treasure. Harmony and Teddy peeked over the covers as the tall, cumbersome fairy retreated out the door.

Harmony flung her pillow back and grabbed a large silver coin.

"You're right, Teddy, that fairy did look a lot like Daddy." Moonlight showed through the side of her shade and glinted off the shiny coin in Harmony's hand. "But that's just magic, you know." Harmony's eyes sparkled.

She snuggled down into bed with Teddy, her treasure held tight in her tiny hand. Harmony drifted off to sleep and into sweet dreams of the candy store.

At six years old, Harmony Gleason was a keeper of the trust.

OLIVER'S OUTHOUSE

Kathy Chencharik

Twelve-year-old Oliver Olson had to go. Unfortunately, so did the other five foster children living with the Wilsons. Not to mention their own three children. Oliver stood in line outside the only bathroom in the house, crossing his legs and wishing there was another bathroom.

"Oliver," Mr. Wilson said, noticing his discomfort. "If you need to go that badly, why not go outside. You do know we live in the country with no neighbors for miles."

Oliver's face turned bright red. He really didn't want to go outside. Nevertheless, looking at the long line waiting to use the bathroom, he realized he had no choice. He stepped out of line and, whispering to himself; he repeated over and over, "I wish I had my own bathroom."

Outside, the sun was shining, and birds were singing as Oliver headed for the woods nearby, still wishing for another bathroom in the Wilsons' house. However, he knew times were tough and doubted they could afford it. After relieving himself, the newest arrival to the Wilson clan decided to take a walk.

His father had been a carpenter, and his mother had worked at a bank, but they had both died in a car crash. With no living relatives, child protective services had placed Oliver into the foster care system.

He thought about his parents as he walked farther into the woods. Soon he noticed a path and decided to follow it. It wasn't man-made, probably made by deer or other animals living in the woods and trampling the vegetation.

Up ahead, Oliver heard the sound of branches snapping. A white-tailed deer came out of the woods. The deer raised its tail like a white flag and ran down the path. Oliver followed, trying to keep up, but the deer was long gone. Soon he came upon a clearing in the woods and spotted a small building in the center. He walked over to it, thinking it was a shed, and opened the door.

"Wow," Oliver said as he peered inside. "This is an outhouse, and a two-seater at that!" The building was in dire need of repair. He got an idea and ran back to the house.

"Mr. Wilson," Oliver said as he bent over and tried to catch his breath.

"Slow, down, Champ," Mr. Wilson said.

Oliver finally stood up and said, "I just wanted to know if I could use some of the wood you have out back. And maybe borrow a hammer, nails, a saw, and some paint."

"What for?"

"I'd like to build a tree house," Oliver said, crossing his fingers behind his back, not wanting to mention the outhouse he had found.

"Sure," Mr. Wilson said. "I know your father was a carpenter. Did you learn to build things from him?"

Oliver nodded

"Help yourself. It's nice to see a young man such as yourself with a plan."

Each day Oliver loaded up a wheelbarrow and brought supplies out to the clearing, and soon the outhouse was as good as new. As time went by, Mr. Wilson noticed there was less of a line to the bathroom. One day he watched as one of the foster kids headed into the woods, and he decided to follow. When he reached the clearing, he burst out laughing. Oliver and the other boy turned toward the sound. They looked as if they'd been caught with their hands in the cookie jar.

"I can explain, Mr. Wilson," Oliver began.

"No need to. I can see what it is, especially since you've painted Oliver's Outhouse in bright red over the door. But I thought you were building a tree house."

"Well, the outhouse was here already. I figured I'd fix it up and we could use it as a second bathroom."

"I had no idea this was out here," Mr. Wilson said.

Oliver picked up a canning jar full of change and handed it to Mr. Wilson. "Plus I started charging the others 10 cents apiece to use it. You can use the money toward adding another bathroom in your house."

Number One

ABOUT THE AUTHORS OF FLASH IN THE CAN

Diane Kane writes short stories and poetry. Her self-published children's book, *Brayden the Brave* is featured at Boston Children's Hospital to help families dealing with medical issues. She belongs to two writers groups and enjoys sharing the love of writing with others. Diane has been published in Goose River Anthology and is one of the co-producers and contributors of *Time's Reservoir*, a Quabbin Quills Anthology. Diane lives in a small rural town in Western Massachusetts and spends her summers on the rocky shores of Maine chasing her dreams of writing.

Kathy Chencharik lives across the road from the Millers River in the North Quabbin area, where she likes to capture wildlife in the lens of her camera. She is a free-lance writer whose poetry, non-fiction, and fiction have appeared in several newspapers, magazines, and anthologies. She won the Derringer Award for best flash fiction for "The Book Signing" in Thin Ice (a Level Best Books anthology, 2010). She earned numerous honorable mentions in Alfred Hitchcock Mystery Magazine's "The Story That Won" contest; eight of which are included in Flash in the Can.

Sharon A. Harmon is a freelance writer and poet. She has been published in *Birds & Blooms, Chicken Soup for the Soul* and *The Uniquely Quabbin Magazine*, as well as numerous other publications. Her second chapbook of poetry, *Wishbone in a Lightning Jar* was recently published and she attends many poetry venues. She lives with her husband deep in the woods of western Massachusetts.

Phyllis Cochran has been writing and publishing stories for over twenty-five years. Her work has appeared in Woman's World, Grit, Purpose, Women Alive, Focus on the Family, Chicken Soup for the Soul and various national and international publications. She has run writers' workshops and taught classes on "Writing for Publication." Her memoir, *Shades of Light*, was published in 2006. Phyllis enjoys spending time with family and friends, caring for her great-grandchildren and walking family member's dogs.

Number One

Number One

Manufactured by Amazon.ca
Bolton, ON

10295460R00070